THE
Bully Biscuit
GANG

THE
Bully Biscuit
GANG

WENDY ORR
MIKE SPOOR

Angus&Robertson
An imprint of HarperCollins*Publishers*

For all the kids facing their own
Bully Biscuit Gang — W.O.

Hannah and Beth — M.S.

Angus&Robertson
An imprint of HarperCollins*Publishers*, Australia

First published in Australia in 1995

HarperCollins*Publishers*
25 Ryde Road, Pymble, Sydney, NSW 2073, Australia
31 View Road, Glenfield, Auckland 10, New Zealand
77-85 Fulham Palace Road, London W6 8JB, United Kingdom
Hazelton Lanes, 55 Avenue Road, Suite 2900, Toronto, Ontario M5R 3L2
and 1995 Markham Road, Scarborough, Ontario M1B 5M8, Canada
10 East 53rd Street, New York NY 10032, USA

National Library of Australia Cataloguing-in-Publication data:

Orr, Wendy
The bully biscuit gang.
ISBN 0 207 18540 9.
I. Spoor, Mike. II (Series : Skinny books).
A823.3

Printed in Australia by McPherson's Printing Group, Victoria.

9 8 7 6 5 4 3 2 1
99 98 97 96 95

It was our first day at the new school. Kirsty
and I didn't think we were going to like it.

'Of course you will!' Mum said.
'You'll make friends quickly.'

Mum always saw the sunny side of things,
but Kirsty and I knew life wasn't that easy.

Then we saw them: the **BIGGEST**,
MEANEST year fives in the whole world.

And they were waiting ...

'What have you got for playlunch?'

I showed them my apple. The biggest girl, Melissa, grabbed it and hurled it into the bushes.

'We don't like apples! Bring us something good
tomorrow, and we might let you have a bite.
What have you got, Shorty?'

Kirsty didn't like being called 'Shorty'.

She was so mad that her hair nearly stood on end.

She yanked the peel off her banana
and held it up to Melissa's face.

Melissa took it and squished it through her
fingers. Then she wiped her hands on
Kirsty's new school uniform.

'Bring something we like,' she said again.

A bunch of kids had come up to see what was happening. They looked friendly, but scared. They didn't say anything.

When the gang had gone, we questioned the others.
'Who are they?' we asked.

They're a bunch of bullies

'The Bully Biscuit Gang! And you'll be in big
trouble if you don't bring them something tomorrow.'

'Something like a packet of chips,' one boy said.

'Or a muesli bar — they might only take half.'

But we knew we were out of luck before we even got home that afternoon. The smell was drifting out over the garden, all the way to the back gate. The smell was *beautiful*.

The smell was chocolate fudge brownies.

17

Mum was pulling them out of the oven as we walked in.

'How was your new school?' she asked.

'Okay,' we said.

'Do you want a cookie? The brownies are for your school lunches, but you can have a glass of milk and one of the others now. I've made five dozen cookies today!'

She calls them cookies because she's from Canada. Kirsty and I call them cookies when we're at home and biscuits when we're at school.

We went out to the garden and climbed up the kurrajong tree. It's our new special place.

'They're not eating my brownie!' Kirsty said fiercely.

'Eat it on the way to school!' I said. 'We'll tell them Mum won't let us have playlunch!'

So the next morning we gobbled up our brownies as soon as we were out of the gate.

We wiped our fingers on the grass and made
sure there wasn't a trace of chocolate anywhere.

The Bully Biscuit Gang weren't sure what to think.

'Our mum said we didn't need playlunch,'
I told them.

24

'We asked for something nicer,' Kirsty explained,
'but Mum said if we didn't want fruit, we didn't
need anything at all!'

Kirsty's smart. That sounded just like a mum.

'That's exactly what she said,' I told them.

Melissa tipped everything out of my lunch box and then threw the box on the ground.

'You better try again!' was all she said.

Kirsty and I walked home giggling.
'We did it!' we kept saying.
'We tricked the Bully Biscuit Gang!'

But Mum had another surprise for us.

'Your school rang up today,' she said. 'They need an emergency teacher for class 5/6 tomorrow.'

'Oh, no!' we groaned.

The last thing we needed was to have Mum teaching the Bully Biscuit Gang!

Next morning we managed to talk Mum into
letting us walk to school by ourselves, so
we could get rid of the brownies.

They didn't taste as good as usual that morning.

We had a funny feeling that we weren't
going to stay out of trouble for long.

We were right. At morning play all anyone could talk about was our mum and her funny accent. Kirsty was getting redder and her hair was getting straighter. If the bell had rung one second later she would have exploded.

Lunchtime was worse.

Mum had shown her class the proper way to write a letter. She'd written on the board:

Dear Mom ...

It was the funniest thing anyone had ever heard — a teacher who couldn't spell 'Mum'. And, she'd called their lunchboxes, 'lunch buckets'!

Kirsty and I thought we'd never make friends now.

But the worst of all was on the way home. That was when Mum told us about the great discussion she'd had with her class, when Melissa asked her how she managed to do all her other jobs.

'I told her it was simple,' Mum said brightly.
'I do what I like best — like cooking. The ironing
mightn't always be done, but at least you two
usually have something nice for playlunch.'

Kirsty and I groaned.

I headed out to the tree and started to plan how we could move back to the city. Maybe I was allergic to living in the country. Maybe I could get a strange disease that would only be cured by moving back into our old house ...

'Taste this!' said Kirsty, sticking a spoon in my mouth.

I opened my mouth without looking.

My mouth was on **FIRE**! There was a flame where my tongue used to be and my throat was like the inside of a volcano.

I ran inside and drank six glasses of water before I could even think about murdering Kirsty.

'It's chilli powder,' she said. 'Isn't it a great idea?'

I thought it was about the most disgusting idea
in the whole world, but my voice was still
on fire and I couldn't say so.

Then I saw what
she meant.

The next day we handed over our brownies nice and peacefully. Melissa got one and the rest of the Bully Biscuits fought so hard over the other one that it finally got stomped on and nobody got it.

While they were fighting Kirsty and I were talking.
There were only ninety kids in the school, and
it didn't take long to talk to all of them.

It took a bit longer to make them believe
we were serious. But finally they agreed.

That weekend, Kirsty and I went into action.

'Mum,' we asked, 'could we do some cooking?'
'Sure,' Mum said. 'Brownies are pretty easy.'

We mixed them up: butter, flour, walnuts, cocoa and eggs. And our secret ingredient.

They looked beautiful. We made thick luscious chocolate icing with a dash of pepper sauce, and cut them into nice big squares.

44

We didn't lick the spoon.

And we didn't scrape the mixture out of the bowl when we made the cod liver oil raspberry slice, or the curried chocolate chip cookies.

We left for school half an hour early on Monday morning. Mum gave us a funny look when she saw our boxes of biscuits.

'I hope you girls know what
you're doing,' she said.

We walked fast, and stopped at the school's front gate. As each kid came in we gave them their playlunch. Everyone had remembered to eat their other one on the way.

A few kids were so scared they looked sick.
A couple more had stayed home.

Melissa was late, so the whole gang had to
wait for recess to collect their goodies.

It was the longest morning of my life. I couldn't think about anything else. When Mrs Johnson saw my spelling test she moved me to the front of the room so I could hear better.

The bell rang.

I was the first out from class 3/4, just like Kirsty from class 1/2. The other kids lined up behind us, looking pale green.

Melissa saw me and rushed over, the rest
of the gang straggling behind her.

'Give me a brownie!' Melissa demanded.

I showed her my biscuits.

Everyone else showed the gang their playlunch.

The Bully Biscuits couldn't believe their luck.

The gang were grabbing for the
biscuits as fast as they could.

My hands were sticky and I wiped
them on my school dress.

Kirsty licked the icing off her fingers like it was the most delicious thing she'd ever tasted.

Her eyes watered, but she kept on watching Melissa as if nothing was wrong!

'The only thing is,' I said, 'you mightn't like them. Mum's on a new health kick.'

'She puts her secret ingredient into everything now,' Kirsty went on. 'It's an old Mohican cure.'

'Nice try!' Melissa laughed.

Melissa took a big bite.
Six other Bully Biscuits took big bites.

Eyes bulged and mouths opened and there
were seven strangled sorts of gasps.

Melissa was the first to move.

If she ran that fast in sport she'd make the Olympic team. She reached the water fountain and didn't stop drinking until Cynthia punched her to get a turn.

Then Lisa pulled Cynthia's hair and there was an all-in brawl till Mrs Johnson came out and said that if they couldn't use the water fountain without fighting they couldn't use it at all.

Since they couldn't have water, some of the Bully Biscuits tried to chase the fire away with raspberry slice and chocolate chip cookies. It didn't seem to make them feel any better.

Their faces became tomato red and they held their throats while making funny gargling sorts of noises.

Kirsty and I looked at each other and grinned. The kids all around us were laughing and hugging each other. We had a feeling we might make some friends here after all.

And we didn't think Melissa and her gang would bother us again.

Besides, they couldn't really be called
the Bully Biscuit Gang any more.

Not when they were sick every time
they saw a biscuit!